The Animal in Me, Too!

Written by **Laurie C. Tye**   Photography by **Thomas D. Mangelsen**

WHEN I AM HAPPY

I am like a swift red fox leaping high in the air.

WHeN I aM SNeaKy

I am like a changing chameleon
carefully walking the line.

WHEN I AM KIND

I am like a snow monkey giving
my best friend a hug.

WHEN I AM CONFIDENT

I am like a mother elephant leading my family through the Savanna.

WHeN I aM SiLLy

I am like a playful puma picking
out cloud shapes above.

WHEN I AM Secretive

I am like a great big gorilla trying hard not to be seen.

WHEN I AM FRIENDLY

I am like a monarch butterfly stopping to say hi to a friend.

WHeN I aM quiet

I am like a big burly bison listening to secrets of the prairie.

When I am Adventurous

I am like an orca whale encouraging others to see the outside world.

WHEN I AM JOYFUL

I am like a yellow-breasted meadowlark singing as loud as I can.

WHeN I aM caLM

I am like a gentle giraffe gracefully grazing in the grassland.

WHEN I AM CONTENT

I am like a black bear cub
not wanting to get down
from the tree.

WHEN I AM SHY

I am like a timid tortoise too afraid to come out of my shell.

When I am Smart

I am like an eager young elk learning from my dad...

Because He Loves Me

more than any animal in the whole world.

SHHHH...
good night animals I am going to bed.

For Bradley who taught our kids the value of hard work,
honesty and integrity. — L.T

For Elsa who loves wildlife and nature. — T.M.

Publisher: Laurie C. Tye
www.writeon3@live.com

Design by: Bud Spencer
SUMO Graphics

Production Location: PRC Book Printing , Guangzhou, China
Date of Production: September 2016
Cohort: Batch 1
Website Info: www.pearlriverchinaprinting.com